DREAMWORKS
GABBY'S DOLLHOUSE

Cat-tastic Heroes to the Rescue!

Adapted by Gabhi Martins

ISBN 978-1-338-64158-5

10 9 8 7 6 5 4 3 2 1   21 22 23 24 25

Printed in the USA   40

First printing 2021

Book design by Two Red Shoes Design

Scholastic Inc.

Today Gabby opened a cat-tastic Dollhouse Delivery. It was two superhero costumes! She wore one and Pandy wore the other.

"We're the Dollhouse Defenders!" she said. "We'll protect the Dollhouse from bad guys!"

Gabby put on her magical headband and sang her special song—the one that makes her tiny so she can enter the Dollhouse.

Gabby and Pandy landed in the kitchen, where Cakey was baking.

"Excuse me," Cakey said, "super-cookies coming through!"

"Wow! Cakey, you're a super-baker," Gabby said.

Suddenly, CatRat the bad guy peeked out and said, "Cookies?!"

CatRat jumped onto the table. "I'm going to trap every Gabby Cat so ALL the cookies will be miney!" he said.

CatRat used his hide-and-seek ray to trap Cakey inside a recipe book.

"Oh no!" Gabby exclaimed. Then CatRat laughed and dashed away!

"How are we going to get Cakey out of there?" Pandy asked.

"First we have to find him!" Gabby said.

They looked in the book and found Cakey on a page filled with smoothies.

"There he is!" Pandy said. He pulled Cakey out with his tail.

"You found me!" Cakey cheered.

Suddenly, a shout came from the music room.

"That sounds like DJ Catnip," Gabby said. "CatRat must be at it again! Let's go!"

"I'm super-stuck!" DJ Catnip cried. CatRat had trapped him with his bungee ray.

Gabby pulled on the bungee cords. When they wouldn't budge, she slipped and fell into the instrument tree.

The red tambourines crashed to the floor. Then the red cords disappeared.

"Look!" Gabby said. "The cords go away when you play an instrument that's the same color as them."

Gabby and Pandy played all the colorful instruments and set DJ Catnip free.

"Thanks, Dollhouse Defenders!" DJ Catnip danced. "Boogie over here and give me a high paw!"

Suddenly, they heard Kitty Fairy calling for help.

"To the Fairy Tail Garden!" Pandy said.

"Nothing personal, Kitty Fairy, but I want those cookies all for myself!" CatRat said as he captured Kitty Fairy in a bubble.

Gabby and Pandy tried to jump after her, so CatRat
shrunk them with his shrink ray.

"Oh no!" Pandy cried. "We'll never reach Kitty Fairy now! We're too tiny!"

Gabby looked at the floating bubbles and had an idea. "Jump with me, Super Pandy!"

They jumped from bubble to bubble until they reached Kitty Fairy. With a big hug, they popped her bubble and set her free.

"Thanks for saving me!" Kitty Fairy said. "Let's fly down."

They landed on the ground safely.

"Now I'll grow you back to normal size . . . with a little Garden Magic!" Kitty Fairy said.

When they were big again, Pandy's stomach rumbled.

"Time for a super-snack," Gabby said. "To the kitchen!"

In the kitchen, they found CatRat.

"Oh no!" he said. "I've shrunk myself with my shrink ray! Now this cookie is way too big!"

"Alright, CatRat. I can grow you back to regular size," Kitty Fairy said, "as long as you promise that you won't do any more bad guy stuff!"

"Alright, alright," CatRat agreed.

"Here's to the Dollhouse Defenders!" DJ Catnip said.

"I'll eat to that!" CatRat said.

CatRat

Pandy Paws

Gabby

Kitty Fairy

DJ Catnip

Cakey Cat

Gabby

Gabby is a gleeful girl with a big imagination. When she puts on her magic cat-ear headband and sings a special song, she can shrink down to go into the Dollhouse and play with all the Gabby Cats.

Pandy Paws

Pandy is Gabby's best stuffed animal friend. He comes alive inside the Dollhouse. He's always ready for a fun adventure with Gabby and often surprises her with a "hug attack"!

CatRat

CatRat thinks he has all the answers and wants to be the hero, which often leads to mischief. But at the end of the day, he always does the right thing.

Cakey Cat

Cakey is the Gabby Cat who bakes the tastiest treats! When he's happy, he shouts "Sprinkle Party!" and spins with joy, releasing a colorful shower of sprinkles.

DJ Catnip

DJ Catnip is the Dollhouse's resident musician. Whether he's playing instruments or trying out new beats, he uses music to get out of troublesome situations or help the Gabby Cats have a cat-tastic time.

Kitty Fairy

Kitty Fairy is a tiny cat with fairy wings. She loves taking care of her friends, and she uses her garden magic to spread joy.